BUNNY ROO, I LOVE YOU

By Melissa Marr
illustrated by Teagan White

Nancy Paulsen Books

an imprint of Penguin Group (USA)

NANCY PAULSEN BOOKS
Published by the Penguin Group
Penguin Group (USA) LLC
375 Hudson Street
New York, NY 10014

USA | Canada | UK | Ireland | Australia
New Zealand | India | South Africa | China
penguin.com
A Penguin Random House Company

Library of Congress Cataloging-in-Publication Data
Marr, Melissa.
Bunny Roo, I love you / Melissa Marr ; illustrated by Teagan White.
pages cm
[1. Babies—Fiction. 2. Adoption—Fiction. 3. Mother and child—Fiction. 4. Animals—
Infancy—Fiction. 5. Parental behavior in animals—Fiction.] I. White, Teagan, illustrator.
II. Title. PZ7.M34788Bu 2015 [E]—dc23 2014028890

Manufactured in China by South China Printing Co. Ltd.
ISBN 978-0-399-16742-3
1 3 5 7 9 10 8 6 4 2

Title and text hand-lettered by Teagan White.
The illustrations were done in watercolor and gouache.

to Kaden from Mama -M.M.

to Mom & Dad -T.W.

When I met you,
you were small
and trembling,
and I thought
you might be
a little bunny.

I held
you close
so you were
warm.

When I tried
to put you down,
you kicked and
squirmed, and
I thought you might
be a lost kangaroo.

I tucked you
in my pouch
so you would
feel safe.

Then one day,
you lifted your head
and looked around, and
I thought you might
be a curious lizard.

I brought you
to a nice, warm
patch of sunlight
so you could
see the world.

Then you opened your mouth and howled, and I thought you might be a lonely wolf.

I ran to my
house and made
you a cozy den
so you had a home.

Then you whimpered
and meowed, and
I thought you might
be a thirsty kitten.

I offered you
some milk so
you would not
be hungry.

Then you yawned
and flopped, and
I thought you might
be a tired piggy.

I gave you
a bath
so you would
be calm.

Then you smiled,
and I knew...

You are not a
bunny-roo-lizard-
wolf-kitten-piggy.
You are my baby.